The Diary of Jenna Mouse

A small mouse with big courage

Joisinga A. Noble

By
Joisinga Noble

Thank you, Mom and Dad,
For reading through
This several times with me!

I love you, Joisinga

June 2013

"Let us not become weary of doing good,
for at the proper time we will reap a
harvest if we do not give up."
Galatians 6:9

Wednesday: December 25, 2002

Diary, Dearest Diary,

Hello, I'm Jenna Mouse! My Aunt Megan ("Nutmeg" as Grandpa calls her) gave you, Dearest Diary, to me as a Christmas gift. I can't wait to share all of my adventures with you.

Not to brag, but they ought to be twice as good as any other mouse's adventures since I am training to be an Emergency Response Mouse (E.R.M.). I should have lots of adventures to write about!

I decided to be an Emergency Response Mouse when my cousin, Ella, told me the story of how she lost her eye because she fell into a bush while running from an owl. Her story established in my heart the need to help mice when things like that happen to them.

I almost forgot, Merry Christmas!!!!!!!!

Mom wants my help finishing a pie, Jenna Mouse

{After the pie, yummy}

I thought Mom meant she was baking a pie and she wanted my help. She really meant she wanted me to help her finish eating a homemade chocolate cream pie! It was delicious!

I can't believe I will be a year old on February 14, ten days after Dad, the rest of his litter, and Joisinga Noble turn three. Valentine's Day, Aunt Julia's 1st anniversary, and my litter's (Rena Emma, Amelia, and Emily) birthday is also on the 14th! As you can tell, February is a busy month for the Mouse family!

Joisinga is Mr. And Mrs. Noble's daughter. Most of the extended Mouse family lives in the walls of the Noble's house.

Unfortunately, the only mouselings that live here in the Nobles' house are my sisters, Aunt Megan's mouselings, and me. But that's better than none!

It's bed time, Jenna Mouse

Friday: December 27, 2002

Diary, Dearest Diary,

In my E.R.M. class today, I learned how to perform mouse to mouse resuscitation. It's much harder than it looks. During class, I told the instructor that I was afraid I might do it wrong in the excitement of an emergency. The instructor reassured all of us that, in the heat of the moment, instinct would take over and we would do what we practiced. I guess that is why we do a lot of practicing!

My cousin, Thomas, married Nora yesterday. It was really funny when the bouquet, which was made of balloon flowers, popped when it landed on a bush. My cousin, Freddie (who is blind and made all the balloon bouquets for the wedding), made another bouquet but decided to have fun and fill it with helium. That one, of course, floated up to the sky. Finally Ella (my cousin and the maid-of-honor) gave Nora hers. Nora's mom, who adopted Nora and is single, caught it!!!!!

The Nobles got a puppy. Her name is Jublulia. Joisinga wanted to name it Julia, but Mrs. Noble (who is Jublulia's mistress) wanted to name her something with either Jubilee (for Christmas time) or Blue (since she's a Blue Pomeranian). Mrs. Noble got creative and merged the 3 into one name.

I have a whole lot of homework to do, Jenna Mouse

Tuesday: December 31, 2002

Diary, Dearest Diary,

Today is New Year's Eve, and tomorrow I will enter into the second calendar year that I have ever lived in, 2003! I am very excited but I think I will miss 2002 a little bit!

In my E.R.M. class, I am now learning how to use a piece of cloth to stop bleeding. It's a little gross! But I guess I will have to learn to deal with it. Fainting is never good in the case of an emergency, especially when you are supposed to be helping!

Goodbye 2002, Hello 2003, Jenna Mouse

Wednesday: January 1, 2003

Diary, Dearest Diary,

Happy New Years! I can't believe it's 2003! Can you? It seems like just yesterday that it was 2002. Oh, wait, it was! These are my New Year's resolutions...

1. Pass the test and become an E.R.M.
2. Move out and into Aunt Gloria's old hole (she moved out when she got married last May)
3. Become a better Christian
4. Help at least 5 mice

Last night I watched the youth pastor of our church, Pastor Jonathan Churchmouse, and Aunt Megan's BFF, Ms. Dorothy Doormouse (Nora's mom), ring in the New Year on the church bells. Aunt Megan was also there watching, and she told me she thinks they are sweet on each other.

It's dinner time, Jenna Mouse

Tuesday: January 7, 2003

Diary, Dearest Diary,

I just found out there will be special guests on January 16th, in our class. The lesson will be about what to do if a mouse goes into labor in an emergency situation. I wonder who the guests will be! Maybe what I learn I can use with Aunt Megan, if she hasn't given birth beforehand.

Yesterday was my cousins' first birthday (Mara, Maria, and Mary). Aunt Megan helped birth them like she did my sisters and me, only they weren't born on a plane like us!

For their birthday, my sisters and I took them to 'Astonishing Cheese Arcade.' They have a Swiss Cheese climbing wall there. It isn't real Swiss Cheese but it looks like it. They also have an 'all-you-can-eat' buffet that includes 17 different kinds of cheese!

My sisters and I are going out to lunch, Jenna Mouse

Friday: January 10, 2003

Diary, Dearest Diary,

Two more months until my final E.R.M. test. If I pass, I will graduate and become a certified E.R.M.

My best friend, Kenna (her real name is Kendra, but she wanted a nickname that rhymed with my name), and I decided to become candy stripers at the hospital until we graduate. Did I mention she is in my E.R.M. class with me? I can't wait to begin our candy striping.

I finished making a cross stich for my hole. It is my birth verse, Galatians 6:9 "Let us not become weary of doing good, for at the proper time we will reap a harvest if we do not give up." Around the verse is a flower vine with flowers in my favorite colors on it; green, light blue, and brown. Amelia saw it and loved it, so I have started making ones for each of my sisters for their birthday with their birth verse and flowers in their favorite colors.

It's time for class, Jenna Mouse

Wednesday: January 15, 2003

Diary, Dearest Diary,

Yesterday was my first day of being a candy striper. It was a lot of fun to cheer up all those hurting mice! I felt really bad for them. So I asked the nurse in charge of the candy striper program if I could do a puppet show for everyone. She asked the doctor she worked under, who asked the hospital director, who told him that was okay. The doctor then told the nurse, who told me. Well, the gist of it is I am doing a puppet show now.

My mom was the first person I told about the puppet show, and then I told my sisters and asked if they would do it with me. They were very excited and immediately started coming up with ideas. When my mom came, in she said, "Sounds like you gals have already begun brainstorming." When we heard that we all had similar thoughts...

Emma took her water cup and splashed it on Rena. Emily and I flashed the lamps we were each sitting by to resemble lightning. And Amelia made a growling noise that sounded a lot like thunder.

After the laughter died down, we heard thunder. I said, "Amelia, the joke is over. You can stop now."

She cried, "It wasn't me!"

Then Emma said with a sheepish grin, "Sorry, that's my stomach telling me it's lunch time." That, of course, sent another wave of laughter!

The show will be geared towards the mouselings, but I think everyone will enjoy it since, in addition to little mouseling humor, we are planning on throwing in some more sophisticated humor.

I will ask my cousin, Thomas, if I can borrow his puppets (he and Nora perform puppet shows at the local orphanage were they used to live before each one was adopted).

It will be great bonding time with my sisters to get to do this together.

We need to go write the play, Jenna Mouse

Thursday: January 16, 2003

Diary, Dearest Diary,

Today's class was defiantly the most exciting one yet!

The special guests were Aunt Megan and Dr. X-Ray (her real name is Xanthia Ray, she is an obstetric doctor)! Everything was going great, and then Aunt Megan went into labor! Good thing Uncle Marty decided to stay and wait for her outside. Kenna went to go get him. He came back in with her but didn't believe her. However, he did believe when he got into the room!

There is a curtain in the room that they used to section an area off for the birth. Then Dr. X-Ray, Aunt Megan, Uncle Marty, and our teacher (Dr. Erma Gensi) went into the curtained off area. Since I am family, I was the only student who got to help. My job was grabbing any medical instruments and supplies that they needed and bringing it to them. What a great way to learn which tools you need!

Some of the other students got a different taste of E.R.M. work today...

Uncle Marty wanted a better view, so he stood on a chair. When the first mouseling started being born, he fainted and hit his head on the top back corner of the chair. He fell backwards through the curtain, landing on the tile floor. He's so talented that he managed not to pull the curtain down with him, so Aunt Megan still had her privacy! Dr. Erma left Dr. X-Ray to care for Aunt Megan, and then she had some of the students help her with Uncle Marty.

Uncle Marty is always clowning around....after all, he is Mr. McClown to the orphans. But I don't think this time was intentional!

When the mouselings were born, I got to be the first one (other than Aunt Megan, Uncle Marty {who was doing better by then}, and the doctors) to see them! Their names are Anne, Annie, Anna, and Ana. Anne was screaming until I held her. She immediately stopped crying and snuggled up close to me. Anne is the same one I got to cut the cord for (Aunt Megan removed all the sacs herself). Anne was so sweet that I didn't want to give her back to Aunt Megan.

Aunt Megan did not have any diapers for the mouselings on her, so the students made them out of the cloth left over from learning how use make cloth to stop bleeding. They used every piece of cloth that was left. Anna (or was it Ana) quickly made use of hers. It sent me on a wild goose chase, but I finally found more cloth in one of the other rooms. Then Aunt Megan and Uncle Marty went home before any of the other mouselings followed Anna's example.

I wish I could have seen my cousin Ella's and the other mouselings' reactions when their parents came home to relieve Ella of her babysitting duties and had four newborn mouselings with them!

I guess I didn't need to use what I learned on Aunt Megan after all, yet I still got to help!

I wonder if this is what it is like to be a real E.R.M. If so, then this will be an adventurous diary after all!

I wish every E.R.M. story ended as happily as this one. Unfortunately, I know that will not always be the case. Hopefully, even if some emergency has an unhappy ending, God will use me to minister to those I meet.

I think I am falling asleep writing, Jenna Mouse

Monday: January 20, 2003

Diary, Dearest Diary,

I started redecorating Aunt Gloria's old hole today. Everyone seems to think we have similar taste; but, after working on her hole, I disagree. I can't wait until I turn one and can move into it because it will be so pretty! Then again, maybe the beauty is in the eyes of the beholder since my sisters all think my color scheme won't look good!

I forgot that Thomas moved his puppet shows to Mondays. The scheduled date of my play is a Monday. So I gathered as many single socks as I could from our family. I had to get rid of the stinky ones (who knew there were so many stinky hind paws in our family)! Now my sisters and I are busy sewing sock puppets, as well as working on the play!

The play is coming along nicely. It's a story and a comedy routine, in one!

I have to give faces to more socks, Jenna Mouse

Monday: January 27, 2003

Diary, Dearest Diary,

Yesterday, during the church service, the youth pastor, Pastor Jonathan Churchmouse, called Ms. Dorothy and her mouselings (through adoption) up to in front of the alter; and they announced they are getting married. Looks like Aunt Megan was right after all!

I have finished two of the cross stiches and have started the next one. Rena's is going to be the biggest cross stitch since her birth verse is Psalms 84:3, "Even the sparrow has found a home, And the swallow a nest for herself, Where she may lay her young - Even Your alters, O Lord of Hosts, my King and my God." That is longer than mine and my other sisters'.

I have noticed that, often after our family dinner, my and my sisters go our separate ways. I use that time to work on their gifts, and I think my sisters are doing the same thing based on their secrecy. Rena usually has paint in her fur. Suspicious, 'fur' sure!

Tonight is family pizza night, Jenna Mouse

Monday: February 3, 2003

Diary, Dearest Diary,

Today is the day of the puppet show (all the puppets are finally done)! I hope all goes well and that it helps cheer the patients up!

Tomorrow is Dad, Aunt Julia, Aunt Stacy, Aunt Margaret, Uncle Alex, Uncle Ben, and Joisinga Noble's third birthday.

At church yesterday, my sisters and I rehearsed our puppet show for the youth group so they could critique it. They all agreed that it was already good and there was nothing left to fix. In fact, Pastor Churchmouse, who also attended our show, asked that we do monthly puppet shows for the mouselings' Sunday school. My sisters said they each have a Sunday school class that they go to at the same time. Kenna was there and piped up, "I can!"

Pastor Jonathan said that would be great. He also said the church already has puppets we could use. There were some really neat ones like a knight with his horse and some that glow under a black light. It will be fun putting together a show with Kenna monthly and then to perform it with her.

Well it's time to go get things set up, Jenna Mouse

{After the show}

The show went great, and everyone was laughing like crazy by the end! I don't think that you could have heard an asteroid drop out of the sky over all the laughter. It sure was hard work, but it was definitely worth every minute! We had twenty puppets in all; and twenty of the patients were mouselings, so we gave one puppet to each mouseling.

I feel bad for Joisinga, tomorrow is her birthday. Her dad is out of state all week for work. He really wanted to be there, and this will be her first birthday without him. Mrs. Noble is taking her out to lunch with all of her grandparents, and then everyone will come back to their home for cake.

It's dinner time (cheesy meatloaf), Jenna Mouse

Monday: February 10, 2003

Diary, Dearest Diary,

Today in class we learned about frostbite and how to help mice that have hypothermia. If they are in the beginning stages of hypothermia (they will probably be shivering), then you can help them by getting them to do jumping jacks or some thing else that keeps them moving. If they have stopped shivering, on the on the other hand, then you want them to keep still to preserve body heat.

Joisinga got Hamtaro playsets for her birthday (Hamtaro is a cartoon series about hamsters). The pieces are just the right size to play with after she goes to bed. There are places to climb, ladders, a see-saw, and a wheel. There is also furniture and other items. When Aunt Megan's mouselings are old enough for me to babysit, we can play on those toys.

Four more days until my litter's and my birthday, Valentines Day, and Aunt Julia's first anniversary!

Busy, busy, busy, Jenna Mouse

Friday: February 14, 2003

Diary, Dearest Diary,

Happy Birthday to me!!!! And the rest of my litter! Happy Anniversary to Aunt Julia and Uncle Ernst! And Happy Valentine's Day to everyone!

I finished all those cross stiches just in time! I framed them with twigs and they look really nice! I hope my sisters agree. Did I mention only Rena is staying in the same house as me. The rest of my sisters are going to live in the house that Mom grew up in and still has family there.

I can't wait to see what my gifts are, Jenna Mouse

{After all the gifts}

We each got some furniture for our holes: sofas, dining room sets, and shelving. Our parents and Uncle Lyle (on Mom's side), who is a carpenter, made the furniture! It's so thoughtful of them; I love it all!

Instead of having us open our presents, Mom, Dad, and Uncle Lyle blindfolded me and led me to my hole where the furniture was (along with most of my other belongings). I had to keep silent while they did the same for each one of my sisters. As each of us got our 'gifts', we got to tag along for the rest of the unveiling. Poor Emily only got to see the unveiling of her hole since she went last.

Then we went back to our parents' hole and had Cherry Velvet Crumb Cheesecake (it's a combination of Joisinga's BeaBea's {her maternal grandmother} recipe and, of course, a Mouse family favorite - Cheesecake!). After the cheesecake was devoured (it was delicious), we sisters exchanged presents.

Rena got flashlights to use as lamps and painted them in our colors. I knew she was up to something - the paint in her fur gave it away! Amelia made pillows for each of use in our favorite colors. Emma made table cloths and place mats in our colors. Emily made us each a rug and a welcome mat using embroidery floss in our colors. Our holes are going to look great with all those gifts!

Time for my first night in my new hole, Jenna Mouse

Friday: February 28, 2003

Diary, Dearest Diary,

Ten more days until I graduate! I have learned so much! I can't wait to start saving lives and helping mice!

My sisters, Emily and Emma, have started courting. I don't want to court, but also don't want to be left on my own trying to find a mouse, so I have asked Mom and Dad if I can try having each of my sisters (and maybe other family members) pick a guy for me to go out with and see how it goes. They said, "Yes".

I am going to make my dinner, Jenna Mouse

Sunday: March 9, 2003

Diary, Dearest Diary,

Tomorrow I can graduate! I am so nervous about that Final Exam! I am going to spend the rest of the night studying with Kenna. Maybe I should set up a table and
some chairs in the hall. Then we can study in the hall and call it "Study hall". I'm just kidding; we will most likely work in the living room or at the dining room table.

Last night, Pastor Churchmouse and Ms., I mean Mrs., Dorothy had a big wedding celebration at church and all the members of the church were invited. I wonder what she thinks of her new last name! I guess she will have to start being really quite – as quite as a church mouse!

I need to get our work space ready, Jenna Mouse

Monday: March 10, 2003

Diary, Dearest Diary,

I am now an E.R.M. I passed the test with 99.999999%! Just joking, I got 100%! So did Kenna. I can't wait until our first emergency (although it would be nice if there were none in the first place).

I got a fancy alarm that is in my hearing range and not in a human's hearing range (that way the Nobles won't be able to hear it). It will ring whenever there is an emergency. I also got a similar portable alarm that is pink to match my purse. When either rings, we go to the fire station where we ride in one of the emergency vehicles (they are actually remote control cars that have been modified and painted) to the scene of the emergency.

Today was my last day as a candy striper. I will miss, it but being an E.R.M. is now my full-time job.

The alarm ringing already, Jenna Mouse

{After the 'emergency'}

I raced down to the fire house as fast as I could. It turned out it was just a test to make sure we would come quickly and to get us used to the alarm. They said there will be test like that every once and a while. Kind of like those fire drills they have at school.

It's been a full day, Jenna Mouse

Saturday: March 15, 2003

Diary, Dearest Diary,

Today the alarm rang really early! I was still in bed, so I yanked off my pajamas and pulled on the first shirt and pants that I found in my closet. I was starved, so on my way out I grabbed a crump I found and ate it as I ran. I was one of the first mice to arrive at the fire station.

We piled into the emergency van and raced to the scene. When we got there, we discovered that a cat had driven a mouse up a tree. The cat followed her up and got stuck. The mouse couldn't get down because the cat was in the way; the cat couldn't get down because she was too afraid.

First we saved the mouse, and then we asked the cat to promise that she would not try to hurt us if we saved her. Since cats are known for going back on their word, we muzzled her in a special muzzle that will slowly dissolve when she at licks it. We lowered it from the branch above to put it on her. The muzzle will take a while to dissolve, buying us more time to get away safely. It is catnip flavored so that cats will want to lick it.

I have learned from this experience and now keep an outfit ready on the chair beside my bed. I also am keeping a large crumb on the table next to the doorway of my hole.

Kenna has invited me for dinner, Jenna Mouse

Friday: March 21, 2003

Diary, Dearest Diary,

Emily and Emma are getting married in a joint wedding!

The last joint wedding in our family, we were born on the plane trip home from Sweden. Does that make us "Air-icans" instead of "Americans"? After all, we were born in the sky! Maybe that's why sometimes we can all be real 'air-heads'! Okay, I'll stop now.

Rena picked out a guy for me, and he came to my hole yesterday. His name is Zuke Keynee. He was nice, but to every dish I made he said, "This is good but nothing like my mother's!" When I told Rena about it today she said, "Strange, he likes every thing I cook for him."

The alarm is ringing, Jenna Mouse

{Midnight}

Some mouseteens had found old tin cans while hanging out at the top of a hill. They climbed into the old tin cans, and one of them pushed all the others down the hill. Then, trying to be a show off, he climbed on top of his can and tried to run on top of it down the hill. He fell off and hit his head on a rock. Most of them had at least one broken bone. There was lots of mending to do. The one who hit his head had to get stitches. They all were able to walk away (some with crutches), and got a strict warning not to do it again!

Tomorrow afternoon I will go to Nora and Thomas' hole to help prepare a picnic. We will eat it at the park to celebrate the end of winter and beginning of spring.

I really need to get to bed, Jenna Mouse

Tuesday: March 25, 2003

Diary, Dearest Diary,

At the picnic the other day, I saved a young mouseling. His parents were not paying attention to him, and he wandered into the parking lot. A human skateboarder was headed the mouseling's way; I snatched him up just in time. I returned him to his parents who were surprised to see me walking up with him – they missed the whole thing as both were busy catching up on work while the mouseling played. His name is Anole. I hope they pay more attention to him from now on.

There was another emergency on the 24th. Some mouselings were playing nutball (it is kind of like baseball but played with nuts and sticks), and a mouse got hit in the head. The mouse got a concussion and went into a coma; luckily, it only lasted a few hours. He stayed at the hospital for 24 hours after he woke, for observation, before they let him go home.

I have been spending most of my free time helping Emily and Emma get ready for their joint wedding. They decided on a western theme. So instead of wedding dresses and suits there will be cowgirl and cowboy outfits. The whole thing will be performed on horseback. I don't mean each mouse will ride a horse; I mean everyone will be on the back of one horse. Hopefully, there will be no 'horsing around' during the wedding.

Yipeeicia, Jenna Mouse

Tuesday: April 1, 2003

Diary, Dearest Diary,

The alarm rang earlier today. It was just a test; they had decided, that since today is April Fool's Day, it would be the perfect day for a test. They also figured that it would help make sure that we would come even if it really seemed like a joke.

While we were still at the fire station, Kenna told me that her mom was pregnant and told her she needed to move out by the time the mouselings were born since their hole is so small. She said she wanted to move in with me.

I stood there a moment in disbelief and then started to mutter, "Fine, as long as you are okay with the guest room."

I got as far as, "Fine" and she interrupted, "Great, I'll help you move your stuff into the guest room, and then we can start painting your room purple for me!"

I was totally shocked. It's not like her to be that bold. When she said, "April Fool's!!!" I sighed with relief. She was not offended by my sigh because she knew she was pushing it with taking my room!

Shortly after I got home, the alarm rang again. It was not a test! A mother mouse had laid her mouseling in a new peanut shell crib. She started freaking out when the mouseling getting red blotches. We washed the mouseling off, and the reaction stopped. It turns out the mouseling was allergic to peanuts.

It was a blessing in disguise that the mother found out this way instead of by feeding peanuts to the mouseling. If the mouseling had eaten it, the reaction would have been much worse.

Yesterday was Amelia's turn to pick out a guy. His

name was Rod Flemming. He was really kind and polite. I think I will go out with him again. They say the third time is a charm, but maybe the second time is, too.

I do believe it is time to play some pranks on my family and friends; it has been too long since I have. Besides, what better time is there for pranks than April Fool's Day. Who will be my first victim, Mom, Rena, Emma, Kenna????? Yes. Kenna, she already April Fooled me!

A-'pranking' we will go, Jenna Mouse

Wednesday: April 2, 2003

Diary, Dearest Diary,

Another day, another emergency.

This time, a mouse was wrestling with her brother and dislocated his arm. She offered to get help, but her brother thought he could get it back in place himself. He just made it worse.

Yesterday I told everyone that I was getting married

on November 14th. And that I would become a stepmother. Everyone was thrilled for me, well, except for my parents, who were upset that they had not met the mouse. Of course, it was just an April Fool's joke! Today I told everyone it was a joke (except for my parents, whom I told yesterday as soon as they got upset).

I went out with Rod again. What happened to his manners!?!?!?!? He slumped in his chair at dinner and burped several times with out saying excuse me. He never said, "Please" or "Thank you." He reached all the way over the table to get the butter. He even blew his nose at the table. That was all just the first half hour.

I am going to head to bed, Jenna Mouse

Monday: April 7, 2003

Diary, Dearest Diary,

Lunch was cut short by an emergency today. This time we were not successful. A mouse was poisoned with a very strong poison. By the time she realized she had been poisoned and called, it was too late. When we got there, she could hardly lift her head. She took me by the paw and asked me to take care of her husband and mouselings. I assured her I would. Moments later she passed away, still holding my paw. Her name was Clara, short for Clarinet. Her husband's name is Mario Micestro.

I went to Rena's house tonight; Zuke Keynee was there. He apologized for what he had said about my cooking and told me that mine was actually really good, yet still not as good as his mom's. Doesn't every guy say that?

He also said that he really liked Rena. When she had asked him to do her a favor, he, wanting to make her happy, said, "Yes." He was very upset when he found out that favor was a date with me. That day, not only was he annoyed at Rena for asking him and mad at himself for not speaking up, but he also wanted to make it so I wouldn't want to go out with him again.

After our date, he told Rena how he felt; and they are now going out. I have to admit Rena's cooking is better than mine, anyway!

I have to help with my sisters' wedding, Jenna Mouse

Monday: April 14, 2003

Diary, Dearest Diary,

This morning, I watched Clara and Mario's mouselings. Their names are Melody, Harmony, Lyrical, Ray, and Major. Their late mother loved to sing and played several instruments (including the clarinet). Their father is a music teacher and plays several instruments, as well. They are a lot of fun, even though they are grieving over the recent loos of their mother. I hope that, if I ever have mouselings, they are just like them.

For lunch, I planned a picnic lunch with Emma's thought-to-be-a-perfect-mouse-for-me, whose name is Terri Cloth. When I mentioned being an E.R.M. he got all upset. He said "a woman should not be an E.R.M. She should leave a man's job to a man," and left. He missed out on my Famous Strawberry Shortcake with cream cheese icing drizzled on top. There is no way he's going to work out; he was really cute, but really not worth it!!!!

That's the alarm, Jenna Mouse

{Much later}

I am so tired. A mouse had the tip of her tail cut off by a lady, who was gardening and accidently cut of her tail, and then ran away when she saw the mouse. The mouse is a model and was very upset. While the other E.R.M.'s stopped the bleeding, I found the tip in the garden. I snuck into the house, found the pantry, got a baggy, and got a piece of ice from the freezer. I put in the ice in the baggy with the tip of her tail.

We took her, and her tail, to the hospital where Dr. Erma Gensi was able to sew the tip back on. Dr. Erma said the model might be blessed and have very little scarring and can be back to modeling in a week. Dr. Erma said I did a great job and kept a cool head (and a cool tip of a tail)!

During this past week, I went to a professional steeplechase chipmunk race. They are like the human/horse steeplechase races. It is a team sport with mice and chipmunks. The mice that ride are very petite, just like human jockeys. The chipmunks are blindfolded so they have to rely on the mice to lead them. There is a meet-and-greet afterward where you can meet the chipmunks and their riders. There are high school, college, and professional levels. We mice don't bet, but we do cheer for our favorites and dress up in the team colors.

Chipmunks, in general, have very interesting names such as Chip off The Old Block, Bright Eyed 'N' Bushy Tailed, Nuts About You, and, the one I rooted for, Candy Stripes. Despite me wearing my old candy striping outfit and cheering as loudly as I could, Candy Stripes did not win. Maybe next time.

I am glad that I was able to help her, Jenna Mouse

Tuesday: April 15, 2003

Diary, Dearest Diary,

I went to see the model at the hospital this morning. The anesthesia had worn off, and she said she felt like herself despite the throbbing pain in her tail, but at least she knew that pain meant it was there. I learned that the model's name is Felicity. Felicity told me she was grateful to be alive. As the hand trowel came down on her, she thought, "This is it; this tool is going to be the death of me. I won't even get to enjoy the asparagus tips I just picked or model in Paris on the beams of the Eiffel Tower." (Mice will often do fashion shows on the wide beams of bridges or places like the Eiffel Tower.)

She was very grateful and wanted to repay me, she insisted even though I told her I was just doing my job. She had come up with the idea of hooking me up with a mouse who is a fashion designer and photographer so I can design my own line and have my own fashion show. She seemed so crest-fallen when I turned down her offer that I rethought my answer. I. M. Fabiomouse is the name of the mouse she is hooking me up with. I will meet him this afternoon.

What a 'tail' I'll have to 'tail' everyone, Jenna Mouse

Thursday: April 17, 2003

Diary, Dearest Diary,

I have been very busy designing the outfits for my fashion show. I showed some of my designs to Fabio (as I. M. Fabiomouse likes to be called), and he liked them but thought they needed more accessories. Who knew you needed so many accessories for one fashion show!

I decided that all the proceeds would go to a homeless shelter. That is, if my designs are good enough that mice want to buy them. The fashion show will be open for both retail and private buyers (and I can invite my friends and family).

When I am not responding to an E.R.M. call, working on a puppet show with Kenna, designing for the show, or helping to get things ready for the wedding, I am watching Mario Micestro's mouselings. I certainly have been a very busy mouse!

Emily says she has a mouse in mind for me. This will be my fourth try.

Mr. Noble's birthday is in two days. He will be 38 years old. Do you know how old that is in Mouse years?!

I just had an accessory idea, Jenna Mouse

Saturday: April 26, 2003

Diary, Dearest Diary,

I went out with Emily's selection today. He is very intellectual... possibly a little too cerebral for me! He conversed with a vernacular utilizing such a plethora of enormous words that I could seldom comprehend that which emanated from his mouth.

I am not an ignorant mouse, but I spent the evening frustrated, confused, and perplexed. I occasionally contemplated if he was trying to obfuscate his communication. I felt inadequate under his scrutiny when, for deficiency of understanding, I could just mutter, "Uh-huh." When he absconded, I expended the next hour perusing the dictionary!

I do not like conversing with sesquipedalian mice (a sesquipedalian mouse is a mouse who likes to use long words). I like the word anthropomorphism, which means to give human like characteristics to animals. Personally, I like to think of it as being the other way around!

Pending we encounter again, Jenna Mouse

Tuesday: April 29, 2003

Diary, Dearest Diary,

There are some new additions to the Noble family pets. Two female gerbils named Snowball and Stuart Little. At first we thought Stuart was a boy. Turns out Joisinga just really liked the name and, being only three years old, didn't care what gender the gerbil was. Stuart likes to be called Lily (short for "Little").

When my Mom met them, she told them the Nobles also have a cat named Mandy but not to worry about her, because she is nice. Snowball's first reaction was, "I'm named after a cat." Poor Snowball!

I'm glad I didn't have to rely on Joisinga to name me – I might be called Hokie like she named her large stuffed mouse!

I asked Mom who I was named after. She said, "Abraham Lincoln." I was trying to figure out how you get "Jenna" from "Abraham Lincoln." Then she said, "Abraham Lincoln was named in 1809; you were named in 2002." Then she seriously told me I was named after my Great-great-great-great-great-great-great (fifty "greats" total) Grandmother Jenna Mouse on Dad's side. How sweet and special.

I think I will go meet the gerbils, Jenna Mouse

Wednesday: May 7, 2003

Diary, Dearest Diary,

Only ten more days until the fashion show! It's on Mr. and Mrs. Noble's 6th anniversary so I picked their wedding colors of pink, white, and blue as my theme colors. I am so excited (and nervous) about the show! I hope I can finish all my designs by the 10th so they can be sewn in time!

My cousins Mara, Maria, and Mary had asked if they could try their hand at picking out a date for me. I said that would be fine if it was okay with Mom and Dad. They gave the okay, so tonight I will go out with the guy Mara chose.

It's the alarm (after a small reprieve), Jenna Mouse

{9:00}

A mouse had been caught by a cat and was quite scratched up. He lost a lot of blood but made it out okay.

When I got home, Miguel (Mara's guy) was there. He was agitated that I was so late but was very understanding once I told him why. He is a nice mouse, but is not a Christian. I don't believe in being unequally yoked. I do think we could become good friends. Maybe I could be a Godly influence in his life.

I should be getting to bed, Jenna Mouse

Friday: May 16, 2003

Diary, Dearest Diary,

The outfits look great, if I do say so myself! I kind of forgot to get models for my outfits until I turned in my dresses on May 10th, and they asked who would be wearing them. I started freaking out that I quickly had to find ten models for the ten outfits in my collection.

I am going to model one of the dresses (of course). I asked my sisters and they agreed to do it, then I asked Mara, Maria, Mary, and Kenna, and they also agreed. I was still one model shy of what I needed so I asked the mouse who made this happen in the first place, Felicity! I also asked her if she would help me style everyone's fur. She accepted and said she was honored that I would ask her.

On May 8th I asked Mario if he and his students could play live music for the fashion show. Trying to be funny he said, "I know the perfect Mousezart piece to play," and started humming it. With a quicker tempo, I thought it was the perfect music for the runway. Many of his students already learned it. He might have been trying to be funny, but it did not fall 'flat', it was really rather 'sharp' of him! I'll give it a 'rest' now.

I was not able to make it to the last steeplechase chipmunk race. Kenna was able to make it, wearing her candy striping outfit, of course; and she said that Candy Stripes won! I can't believe I missed it!

I still have to go decorate the stage, Jenna Mouse

Sunday: May 18, 2003

Diary, Dearest Diary,

The show was a huge success. We got orders for a total of 500 complete outfits including the accessories! Who knew I was so talented when it came to fashion? I guess that is just one of the hidden talents God gave me. Maybe I should do this sort of thing more often!

My favorite outfit was a pink mini dress with a blue belt and white jean capris tights; it had a matching blue beret, white purse, and blue sandals. That one sold the least, but my second favorite sold the most.

I noticed I. M. Fabiomouse flirting with my cousin, Ella. I think she was flirting back in her own sort of way by telling him all about when her mom's fashion designer friend, Laija, came from Sweden to visit last summer. Ella told him how she was interested in being a fashion designer and about some of the designs she sketched. Fabio said that it sounded like they might have similar tastes and might make a great fashion designing team. Do I sense a mutual attraction?

Amelia invited Rod Flemming to the fashion show. After the show, Felicity, he, and I talked. He burped loudly and interrupted several times during our conversation. Felicity asked him to go out with her. After he left, I asked her if she minded his poor manners as she is a very well mannered mouse. She said she didn't even notice, that she was the only girl out of two litters, and many of her brothers act the same way. Maybe two couples are in the works…

My stomach is telling me it's dinner time, Jenna Mouse

Saturday: May 24, 2003

Diary, Dearest Diary,

Kenna and I went to 'Charming Chiquita's' after I left Mario's hole. Kenna grabbed my arm, pointed to the display window, and started shrieking, "Those are the outfits you and I wore for your fashion show!" When we got inside, I saw that they had all ten of my outfits for sale. I still can't believe that they bought any of them, let alone all ten!

To make things even more exciting, we saw a woman buy the pink mini dress outfit; in fact, when she got out of the store she took the beret out of the bag and put it on!

'Charming Chiquita's' was also where Aunt Megan met Uncle Marty, well, sort of! He was dressed as a clown, and she was acting like a clown. It was months later before she found out her dental hygienist was that clown. Now 'Charming Chiquita's' has special meaning special to both of us.

Good thing the mouse who bought my outfit didn't try to balance the bag on her head like Aunt Megan did! I'd have hated to see my favorite outfit fall and get dirty.

André Wright (the guy who Maria picked out for me) and I went out for coffee and dessert this evening. I think he might be my "Mr. Wright." I just met him, and I already like him. Our Christian views are very similar.

There goes the alarm, Jenna Mouse

Sunday: May 25, 2003

Diary, Dearest Diary,

Last night was another case of mouse poisoning. This time we got to her soon enough, and it was not as strong of a poison as what Clara was poisoned with. The mouse was not in critical condition but ended up being allergic to the anti-poison. She is still in the hospital, and I will continue praying for her.

At church they announced they needed Wednesday Night Youth Group leaders this summer. After the service, Kenna and I talked; and we each had thought it would be fun to lead a class but that we couldn't handle it on our own. Then we burst out laughing. We couldn't handle it alone, but we could certainly handle it together.

We will start on the 4th of June. We have to come up with three field trips that the class can do on Saturdays. We will talk to the head of the E.R.M. program and ask for Wednesday nights and the Saturdays of the field trips off, before we commit to it.

I watched Mario's mouselings again today after church. After he got home, he invited me to stay for some homemade pizza and ice cream. After that we played a quick board game and Melody won. It was really nice. I hope we can do it again.

Some coffee cake sounds good right now, Jenna Mouse

Tuesday: May 27, 2003

Diary, Dearest Diary,

I went out with André today for a longer date. Getting to know him better has convinced me that he is not my "Mr. Wright", after all. Well, I guess he is still Mr. Wright but not "Mr. Right."

I hope Mary's choice works out. If not, I will be left on my own! I am praying that if it doesn't work out God will lead me to the right mouse. Maybe that mouse is right under my whiskers, and I don't even know it!

Yesterday, I received the profits from sale of the

outfits and accessories. I received $25 for each complete outfit plus matching accessories; that's $12,500 dollars! I gave it to the homeless shelter. They were thrilled as they did not know how they were going to pay their bills since they operate off of donations. That was everything they needed, and more! They said it was enough for a year of expenses. So instead of worrying about closing in a month, as it looked like they were going to have to, they can stay open at least another year. Wow! God sure used me to bless them!

Kenna and I now have Wednesday nights off. I think the homeless shelter might be a good place to take the mouseteen Youth Group for a field trip. Maybe we can also help fill some of the other needs they have by reaching out to the rest of the church for donations.

I watched Mario's mouselings today; they always have good things to say about their father. I can see why – he is so kind to them, and to me, too.

Dinner is ready, Jenna Mouse

Sunday: June 1, 2003

Diary, Dearest Diary,

This morning at church, Miana, one of the mouseteens, told us how her little sister, Tiana, had watched one of our puppet shows at Sunday school and came home from it all excited telling her family every little detail about it, including the lessons she learned.

One lesson (which was not the lesson we intended) was you should cross stitch Bible verses – because you "read what you sew." The lesson was "you reap what you sow", but with all the cross stitches I have done, I know her interpretation is true, too.

Miana said she would love to learn to be a puppeteer and help mouselings learn about God. Her best friend, who was right there, said she would, too.

Right then I had an idea for our class and our three field trips. We could do puppet shows for the local homeless shelter, hospital, and orphanage (if Thomas and Nora don't mind; after all, it is their personal way of giving to all those mouselings). Kenna loved it, so we started planning right away.

Looks like Miana and her best friend will get their wish. That is, if they choose to be in our class. I hope many of the other mouseteens like puppets, too.

I got so excited I forgot all about lunch!, Jenna Mouse

Friday: June 6, 2003

Diary, Dearest Diary,

The tenth is Emma and Emily's wedding date! There is still a lot to do! We have found a horse to hold the wedding on (I never thought I would be saying that)!!!! She is an appaloosa with a gorgeous spotted coat and a striped mane. Emma and Emily finally stopped arguing and picked the outfits. Mine is a pink denim skirt with a blue puffy-sleeve shirt and a pink denim vest (I forgot to mention: I am one of Emma's bridesmaids). I also have a pink cowgirl hat and a pair of pink cowgirl boots.

Our first Youth Group meeting was two nights ago. Miana and her best friend were the first two to show up. In fact, they were waiting on us to arrive!

I asked if any of the mouseteens had puppets, and one of the boys said his grandmother had given him ten of her old mouselinghood puppets and, if we treated them with respect, we could use them. That is perfect since we have ten students. We will spend the next few classes writing it as a group, practicing it, and memorizing it. We will do a practice run for the family members (aunts, uncles, cousins, and grandparents included) the Wednesday before the first performance.

We will do the homeless shelter first, so at tonight's meeting I helped the mouseteens make posters to hang around the church asking for donations of clothing and food. We will give the things we gather to the homeless shelter after the puppet show.

My sisters and I are going to a movie, Jenna Mouse

Sunday: June 8, 2003

Diary, Dearest Diary,

Ella and Fabio have started designing a fashion line

together. I had to rescue a mouse's tail to do a fashion line with Fabio; Ella just had to flirt!!!!!

I was telling Amelia about André Wright, and she said he sounded like the perfect mouse for her. I set them up on a date. The next day, after going on that one date, on the way to church to see the pastor, they picked up their parents and then eloped.

That was yesterday. Mom and Dad told my sisters and me about it after they got home from the ceremony. Amelia and André will go on their honeymoon after Emma and Emily's wedding. Amelia already always thinks she's always right; now she will have the name to back it up with! I wonder why Mom and Dad didn't say that they cantaloupe. (Get it? cantaloupe - can't elope)

I am in disbelief!, Jenna Mouse

Tuesday: June 10, 2003

Diary, Dearest Diary,

Three-fifths of my litter is now married!!!!!!!! Everyone

had a lot of fun at the wedding... except for two of the mice who found out the hard way that they were allergic to horses.

I noticed the first mouse when I started hearing loud 'Achoo's.' Good thing, I always have a medical kit in my purse. I was able to give the mouse some allergy medicine.

Then Emma's maid-of-honor broke out in hives. We had to quickly get her off of the horse. Once on the ground, I gave her a shot; and she soon recovered but stayed off of the horse. The brides and grooms waited until those of us who were helping her got back on the horse to finish their vows. I filled in for Emma's maid-of-honor.

I'm going to nap before the reception, Jenna Mouse

Wednesday: June 11, 2003

Diary, Dearest Diary,

This morning, I went out for breakfast with the guy

who Mary chose, Archie. All throughout our conversation, he put his family and other mice down. I couldn't stand it! It was just plain disrespectful, and I spent the whole time wondering what he would tell others about me! I told him that I didn't feel comfortable with him talking like that; and he just said, "Lighten up, kid."

All these guys have been kinda cute; and with most of them, I can see the initial similarities between us. But I can't believe that my family couldn't see that deeper within we really clash.

I have to go to Youth Group, Jenna Mouse

Sunday: June 15, 2003

Diary, Dearest Diary,

Today was my first time saving a pet mouse. The owners were on vacation. The human, who was supposed to take care of the house, forgot to give the mouse food and water. The mouse was severely dehydrated but should be back to normal by the time his owners get home.

We moved the bag of food next to where the mail was being stacked. Hopefully, the human will get the hint. I will check in on the mouse tomorrow just to make sure. I'm glad I don't have to rely that heavily on humans!

Today Mario asked me out! My brain flew out the window at that moment; and I said, "Yes." Maybe the right mouse was right under my whiskers after all!

Sometimes when we talk, he mentions the mouselings' need of a good Christian mom to help raise them. He has also said he can see my Christian values in my speech and actions. I know he is a mouse who is serious about 'date for mate', looking towards marriage. I know it would be a big responsibility to enter into marriage with a mouse who already has mouselings. But, I do like that he is not looking to date just for the fun of it and that he has strong Christian values.

We decided for our first time going out we would go to his parents house with the mouselings, and if we decide to go out again it would be with my parents. If a third time, with Clara's parents since I would be a step-mom to their grandmouselings. That way we can get to know each other's families, and they get to know us.

Squeak, Squeak, Jenna Mouse

Monday: June 23, 2003

Diary, Dearest Diary,

Mario's family is very nice; I think I would enjoy having them for in-laws (although we are a long way away from marriage)!

While we are a long way from marriage, Rena and Zuke aren't... They are now engaged and will get married on the 21st of next month.

I heard the most beautiful poem today...

Cheese, Cheese, Beautiful Cheese.
Oh, so creamy. Oh, so sweet.
White or yellow, it can't be beat!
I eat it in the morning; I eat it right a noon.

I eat it in the evening and underneath the moon!

Cheese, Cheese, Beautiful Cheese.
Cream cheese, blue cheese,
Can I have some more please?
I love the spice in Monetary Jack.
And each hole of Swiss cheese, front and back!

That poem makes me hungry, Jenna Mouse

Friday: July 4, 2003

Diary, Dearest Diary,

There were lots of emergencies today, almost all of them related to firecrackers. Next year, in June, I am going to do a speech on the dangers of firecrackers. Hopefully, it will prevent a lot of injuries.

Mario, his mouselings, my parents, and I all went marble bowling the last. We decided that it was a great way for Mario and my parents to get to know each other since you can talk when it's not your turn, plus it kept the mouselings occupied.

None of the mouselings were very good at bowling, so they were playing to see who could get the least amount of points without hitting a gutter ball. I won, and I didn't even know I was competing!

I can tell that my parents really like Mario.

On July 1st we had a cookout with Clara's parents and played a bunch of old fashioned outdoor games, like horse shoes, except we use chipmunk shoes. Speaking of horse shoes, do you know why horses don't play horse shoes? Their parents get upset when they throw their clothes around!

I am going to go enjoy safe fireworks, Jenna Mouse

Thursday: July 10, 2003

Diary, Dearest Diary,

During the July 4th fireworks, Mario and I talked and decided to make our relationship more serious and only see each other. I really think he might be the mouse for me!

The mouselings didn't seem as thrilled as we were when we told them about our decision. In fact, the last time I watched them I found a realistic plastic cockroach on my dinner plate (do you know how huge those things are to mice?)! It reminded me of the frog in Maria's pocket in the "Sound of Music"! I hope they adjust to the idea of Mario and I as a couple.

The alarm rang yesterday, but it was just a test. It also rang today. This time a mouse got burned really badly by scurrying along an un-insulated hot water pipe.

Last night was the family puppet show at Youth Group. Ed, the sesquipedalian mouse I went out with, was there. Turns out, he is Miana's uncle. He said to me, "I am one of the components of the mishpocha of Miana."

After the show, Kenna came to my house for a girl's night and sleep over. She said, "Did you meet Ed? He was so charming when he said, 'Your ocular orbits obtain vivacity comparable to that of an Andalusite reflecting the solar radiance' to me." Who knew she was one to fall for those with big vocabularies!?!?!?!?! I wonder if she will start calling her eyes "Andalusite colored" instead of just brown.

The Nobles are going on a cruise in September with Mrs. Noble's parents. I have already gotten approval from the E.R.M. director for that week off, and I will go with them.

I am going to get some shopping done, Jenna Mouse

Sunday: July 13, 2003

Diary, Dearest Diary,

The puppet show went great yesterday, and the mouseteens loved it every bit as much as the audience at the homeless shelter did. The homeless shelter really appreciated the donations. When I showed up with Kenna and the mouseteens, they recognized me as the mouse that gave them the $12,500.

We will do the next puppet show on July 26th at the hospital, where Kenna and I worked as candy stripers. The mouseteens will make simple sock puppets during the next two Youth Group meetings to hand out to the mouselings. We had sorted through the clothing donations for the homeless shelter and found 15 pairs of socks with at least one of them having holes. Kenna has a button collection she has been looking to get rid of, and I have lots of short pieces of ribbon and yarn that we will bring for the mouseteens to use.

We found, while making the posters, that if the mouseteens' paws are busy they are more open to talking and asking questions, making for some great Biblical conversations. I think it's because they are not sitting at a table and staring at each other. Having their eyes on their projects makes them more at ease and less conscience of what others are thinking.

Off to buy the needles and thread, Jenna Mouse

Thursday: July 17, 2003

Diary, Dearest Diary,

Ella proposed to I. M. Fabiomouse! Ella did a fashion shoot of herself holding a man's engagement ring. She then enlarged her favorite and made it look like a magazine cover. She titled the fake magazine cover 'Fashions of Love'. Next to her holding the ring, it had the caption "Will You Marry Me?"

She got the idea from the one Mrs. Noble did to propose to Mr. Noble. The framed 'magazine cover' hangs above Mrs. Noble's side of the bed.

Ella and Fabio are going to get married during their fashion show (with the line they've been working on). The date is July 31st. They, and the rest of the wedding party, will wear the designs since their line includes outfits for both men and women.

Today, there was a hedgehog quill on my seat at dinner (I was eating at Mario's hole). Good thing I noticed it before sitting down! This is sounding too much like the "Sound of Music."

Then, after dinner, the mouselings started telling me these stories about how their Mom loved sneaking up on the cat, pulling its whiskers, and then running away. She also used to find stones with fresh snail slime and use them as a slip and slide for the mouselings and herself. They wanted to know if I would do things like that with them. The slip and slide idea actually isn't bad, but the cat one sounds too dangerous (I'm too busy saving mice that do things like that, to do them myself!).

Kenna told me that she and Ed have begun an exclusive dating relationship. I have noticed her vocabulary growing bigger. I wonder if she is trying to impress him, or if he is just rubbing off on her!

I think I will do some scrapbooking, Jenna Mouse

Monday: July 21, 2003

Diary, Dearest Diary,

Rena Mouse is now Rena Keynee. They had a food item that they requested for each family member to bring to the wedding. It was all for a recipe that Zuke created. He wouldn't tell us its name until after it was made. I brought tomatoes (that turned out to be for pasta sauce). Zuke brought zucchini, of course. Then, after the wedding, following Zuke's directions we made pasta from scratch as a family. Its name is 'Renakeynee.' Just think, if he had kept going out with me it might be 'Jennakeynee.'

I can't wait for the cruise. I started packing and then needed something from what I had packed. What I needed was at the bottom, of course, so I ended up unpacking it all! I just put it all away.

I am full from all that Renakeynee, Jenna Mouse

Thursday: July 24, 2003

Diary, Dearest Diary,

Today there was another emergency. A mouse was climbing up some shelving and fell. Then a cat figurine fell off the shelf sending shards of porcelain all over. We had to be careful around the shards. Many of the mouse's bones where broken, and she had many cuts. But she survived.

As soon as I got home, the alarm rang again. That time a mouse got caught in a mouse trap. I made a silly move and used my paw to lift the metal bar on the trap off of his tail. The mouse got out, but no one was holding on to the wood base under the mouse, so when he got out, the wood snapped up to the bar my paw was holding. It was my right paw and I am right-pawed.

I felt ridiculous when I, an E.R.M., was sitting there getting bandaged up along with the other mouse!

My paw is in a big bandage, so I have to use my left paw to do things. As you can see, I don't write very neatly with my left paw... the sooner I get that bandage off, the better. It will probably be a month, or so, before it heals enough for that to happen.

I didn't finish my sock puppet, and I can't sew now. Kenna is such a good friend; she is done with hers and said she would finish mine for me.

Now I know how Mr. Noble felt last month when he wrecked his motorcycle in West Virginia and broke some ribs!

I think I will try to bake cookies, Jenna Mouse

Saturday: July 26, 2003

Diary, Dearest Diary,

The play went well, and the mouselings loved the sock puppets. There was just enough so that each of the mouselings at the hospital could get two.

I have asked Thomas and Nora, and they said that we could do a puppet show at the orphanage in two weeks.

At the next Youth Group meeting, the mouseteens will make posters asking for donations of Scampers diapers (it's the only disposable diaper brand available for mice), lightly used (unbroken) toys, and mouselings' clothing.

After trying to baking those cookies, I figured out that I couldn't really bake or cook one-pawed, so Rena has been making my meals for me. Good thing for me that instead of going away for a honeymoon, they are working together on enlarging her hole here in the Noble's home.

Rena is here to make dinner, Jenna Mouse

Thursday: July 31, 2003

Diary, Dearest Diary,

Ella and Fabio's wedding was really cool. Everyone in the wedding party, including the pastor, walked down the runway like models; and it was like a normal fashion show. Then during the grand finale everyone got into position at the head of the stage, and the wedding began. I. M. Fabiomouse is wealthy, so everyone at the wedding got an outfit from the fashion line as a surprise! I got a beautiful purple evening gown, complete with long matching purple gloves (Ella also made a third glove for tonight to fit over my bandage), that I wore to the reception.

The photographer took a bunch of pictures of me because she mistook me for the maid-of-honor, who was wearing the same gown and gloves, and has the same colored fur. The photographer was really good, she worked hard to capture as much of the event as possible. Her name is Stephie Pozey. I can't wait to see how the photos.

I am going to read a book, Jenna Mouse

Saturday: August 2, 2003

Diary, Dearest Diary,

"August" of wind just breezed by (that was a joke).

I can't really clean the house well, so Kenna has been helping me. One day, while she was doing my laundry, she pulled out my favorite pair of jean capris. They had a huge rip in them that was not there before she did the laundry. I was very upset; I had kept that pair nice since I was a mouseteen. They were long jeans on me back then, before I had my last growth spurt, which was of a whole centimeter. After that they became capris on me.

When Kenna saw how upset I was, she told me that it was actually her matching pair that she had ripped on a toothpick. I forgot how much she loves a good joke – that was not a good joke in my opinion. Good thing for her that we are best friends…. and that I need her help right now!

I am starting to get better at doing things with my left paw (although my writing hasn't improved). I still am looking forward to the day when I can use my right paw again!

I am currently off duty as an E.R.M. (due to my accident). I found that I kind of miss the excitement! Kenna is updating me on the latest news and emergencies. Last night a mouse fell into a ditch and couldn't get out without the help of the E.R.M. team.

I think I will read another book, Jenna Mouse

Sunday: August 10, 2003

Diary, Dearest Diary,

This play was the best yet. The mouseteens improve with every play. I am disappointed that this is the last one. The orphanage appreciated the donations. The mouselings loved it more than all of Nora and Thomas's plays put together... just kidding. They did really enjoy it.

These days are going slowly by. I have watched Mario's mouselings quite a few times. They tell me about all these crazy things their mother did that they hope I will do, too, if I marry Mario! I think getting my hand caught in a mouse trap was crazy enough for me! Being married to a mouse like that seems out of his character, but I guess it must be true what they say about opposites attracting.

Well, Rena is coming with pizza, Jenna Mouse

Wednesday: August 20, 2003

Diary, Dearest Diary,

I spend most of my time reading since I have nothing else to do. I have read fifteen thick books since the accident! Each one is a centimeter thick, do you know how many pages that is?

I go to the doctor in four days so he can look at my paw and see how the healing has progressed. If it all goes well I can get the bandage off then!

Counting the days, Jenna Mouse

Monday: August 25, 2003

Diary, Dearest Diary,

The doctor said that I should come back in a week for him to check it again before removing the bandage. Hopefully I will survive until then!

I have not had an official date with Mario in over a month, but I have watched his mouselings many times. Some of those times I have stayed for dinner, a board game, their family devotions, and then help put the mouselings to bed. After they are in bed I will spend up to two hours talking with Mario.

On evenings like that, I almost feel as if I am family. And who knows, that may not be too far from the truth soon! Only time will tell for sure.

I went to the steeplechase chipmunk races with Kenna the other day. We both got to ride on Candy Stripes; the chipmunks gave a short ride to anyone dress in the colors!

'The sun will come out tomorrow', Jenna Mouse

Thursday: August 27, 2003

Diary, Dearest Diary,

Tonight is the last Youth Group meeting. I will miss them and doing the class; but, at least, Kenna and I still have the monthly puppet shows for the mouselings' Sunday school.

We are having a party for our class tonight. There will be cake, snacks, and punch. Kenna and I put together a scrapbook with pictures Kenna took over the past three months. She took a lot of pictures of all our meetings, the family puppet show, and the three field trips. We will have the scrapbook out on a table for whoever wants to look at it.

I hoped they had fun this summer, and more importantly, learned something (other than just being a puppeteer and making posters)!

It is about time to leave, Jenna Mouse

Monday: September 1, 2003

Diary, Dearest Diary,

It's off!!!!!!!!!!!!!!! My paw is still a little sore and tender, but it should be back to normal soon.

I am so glad that I can do things again, but I will miss Rena's cooking (she is a good cook)! She taught me a lot of her recipes while I sat watching and talking as she cooked. I enjoyed hanging out with Kenna, too. She was a big help with all my chores, including dishes. Every meal became an adventure for Rena and me; we were constantly guessing where Kenna stashed the cooking utensils – it was in different places most times.

I will start back to being an E.R.M. in a week. I'm glad because I like to be where the excitement is at!

Kenna says she thinks Ed might propose to her soon. I can't imagine having him as a "best friend-in-law".

I am going to celebrate my freedom, Jenna Mouse

Monday: September 8, 2003

Diary, Dearest Diary,

Today was Mrs. Noble's birthday! I hope it was a happy day for her!

Kenna was right; Ed proposed to her last night. This morning, I went to Kenna's hole to help her begin her wedding planning. The wedding will be on the 30th of this month. Wow! Was that quick or what?

I am going to look for cake crumbs, Jenna Mouse

Wednesday: September 10, 2003

Diary, Dearest Diary,

I am back on the job. I know because the alarm rang today and woke me up from the sweet dream I was having about Mario. This time a mouse had a rock land on her. She didn't make it.

Today when I got to Mario's hole the mouselings were

crying. Apparently, Mario had found out about the lies they had told me about their mother; and, after a long talk, the mouselings decided that they wanted this relationship between Mario and I, after all. They told me that all those things that they had said their mom used to do were made up stories used to try to keep me away. They also apologized for the plastic cockroach and hedgehog quill.

With the mouselings finally okay with our relationship, Mario and I decided to get married!!!! It was not a fancy wedding proposal, but he did get down on one knee. The mouselings all cheered and hugged me. Harmony went to her room and came back with a party popper (thrown away after a party the humans in their house had). The mouselings all had to pull on the string to make it pop, putting confetti all over Mario and I. (Mario was making them clean it up as I left).

I can't believe my best friend and I got engaged just three days apart. Who would have thought it?

The cruise is just four days away. Now I will start packing (again).

Out to dinner with my soon to be family, Jenna Mouse

Sunday: September 14, 2003

Diary, Dearest Diary,

Wow, I have never seen the ocean! It is so cool! The ocean reminds me of the hymn "Love Lifted Me." It starts out "I was sinking deep in sin, far from the peaceful shore." I do hope this is a peaceful trip…..

Joisinga brought some toy motorcycles, and I can ride them after she goes to bed. My favorite is the red sport bike - the only thing that could make it better is if it had a motor!

There is so much to do on this cruise ship. There is putt-putt, swimming, exercise facilities, ice skating, art auctions, bingo, and live shows to watch. Not to mention food available nearly 24 hours in many places and many different kinds of food!

I think I will start with ice skating. I bet I could do a figure eight, or maybe I should just get the actual skating down first!

I hope I don't get sea sick, Jenna Mouse

Wednesday: September 17, 2003

Diary, Dearest Diary,

Mr. Noble wrecked the red sport bike! That's the second motorcycle wreck this year for him. At least, this time he didn't break any bones. He and Joisinga were playing with it on the balcony ledge, and it fell into the ocean!!! I guess he made some fish very happy (ha, ha)!

Oh well, I guess I'll just have to find a new favorite and hope it doesn't get wrecked! As long as I keep it away from Mr. Noble that should not be a problem. I am just kidding; he really is a nice human.

A very sad mouse, Jenna Mouse

Saturday: September 20, 2003

Diary, Dearest Diary,

Tomorrow we arrive back home; I'm really going to miss this cruise. I have kept myself busy ice skating, riding motorcycles, and shopping (not to mention eating the delicious food crumbs). I've gone to an active volcano, the beach (where Joisinga held a little live starfish, and I rode on one), a cocoa bean farm, a cave, and many other places!

Joisinga's been taking pictures with the cutest little camera. The camera is decorated as a block of cheese, and there is a mouse lens cover – the mouse slides over to expose the lens.

Often I will sit with my sketchbook and draw pictures of the scenery and places I have seen. I am not the best artist; but. at least. I can recognize what I draw!

This week away from the Micestros has really made me miss them! My feelings make me even more certain of our love! I got a variety of sea shell souvenirs for each of the mouselings. For Mario, I got a beautifully paw-painted set of maracas.

I am going to enjoy the rest of this trip, Jenna Mouse

Monday: September 22, 2003

Diary, Dearest Diary,

We're goin' to the chapel, and we're gonna' married. Goin' to the chapel, and we're gonna' married. Goin' to the chapel, and we're gonna' married. Goin' to the chapel of love! ♪ ♥ ♪

After I got back from the cruise, Mario and I set a date for the wedding - November 14th. It suddenly feels so real now that we have a date.

Now Kenna can help plan my wedding, like I did with hers. I now know how she felt with the excitement of her wedding in the air.

I need to book Stephie Pozey to be our wedding photographer! The photos she did for the Fabiomouse wedding turned out wonderfully, even the ones of me as the 'maid-of-honor imposter'. Some of the photos looked like fashion shoots; and others like the typical wedding poses; and some just candid of the friends and family.

I am going to look at wedding dresses, Jenna Mouse

Tuesday: September 30, 2003

Diary, Dearest Diary,

Kenna is now married; I can't believe it! The vows were romantic; at least I think they were... I could hardly understand them. They contained so many large words I thought they were in a different language! At least the vows sounded pretty. It was a good thing for me that I could understand parts I was needed for, or else I would have done a lousy job of being her maid-of-honor!

I suppose I should go to bed, Jenna Mouse

Saturday: October 4, 2003

Diary, Dearest Diary,

I picked out my dress. It's a simple cream-colored old fashion one with a high lace collar, lace shoulders and sleeves, tiny pearl buttons down the back, a princess cut waist, and a plain long satiny skirt. I also got a veil made of the same lace. It has pearls, which are very similar to the buttons, all around the veil and extra pearls on the headband part of the veil.

Mario said he would leave the wedding planning up to me, as he had started planning his first wedding and it was a bit of a catastrophe until his wife took control.

I decided our wedding theme should be old fashion; we will even do some wedding photos in sepia. We are having it in an old chapel that is no longer used for church services but is rented out for weddings. Since there will be no human weddings there on that day, we will hold it on one of the uncushioned pews.

Fabio, Ella, and I are going to design the outfits for all of Mario's mouselings.

The reception food will be tea, biscuits, finger sandwiches, mini wedding cakes, as well as a small wedding cake. The mini cakes will be shaped like teacups, and the bigger one will be shaped liked a teapot. Mario and I came up with our own tea blend of white tea leaves, white peach, apple, and a hint of cinnamon. It smells and taste delicious; I hope our guests agree.

I just realized that Mario and I have not picked out our rings yet. How could I forget? - I'm a girl!!!! I will talk to him when I watch his mouselings tomorrow.

Wedding planning makes me hungry!, Jenna Mouse

Sunday: October 12, 2003

Diary, Dearest Diary,

The alarm was out of order. It was ringing every hour for no reason. I spent several hours running to the firehouse and back. I didn't know what to do! I finally took it to the fire station where they fixed it. I am so thankful!

It is ringing; I hope it's not broken again, Jenna Mouse

{I'm back}

It was for real! A mouse had used a plastic grocery bag as a parachute. It didn't work right; he hit his head and then started suffocating when the bag landed on top of him. Another mouse, who got there before we did, used mouse to mouse resuscitation while his wife ran for help. The mouse survived but has a bad head injury.

Mom and Dad are making dinner, Jenna Mouse

Saturday: October 18, 2003

Diary, Dearest Diary,

Things have been pretty uneventful. My days are full of getting ready for the wedding, watching Mario's mouselings, on-call for E.R. M., and, well, not much else!

The wedding preparations are coming along nicely. Though, at first, they weren't! Fabio and I kept arguing over the designs. He designs more modern things. He said that he knew nothing about any old fashion styles, therefore he wanted to make the mouselings' outfits more modern. I, on the other hand, wanted to stick with the old fashion theme. Ella was willing to try her paw at old fashion. I had to search for something to show him what I wanted.

Finally, I found some pictures of my great-great-great-great-great-great-great (fifty "greats" total) grandmother Jenna's wedding which was in 1899. After that, we were able to work together quite well (with only a few minor problems).

All the men have old fashion suits with long tails (on their suits). Squeaking of tails, all us girls will wear bows on our tails. The colors are pink and rustic brown.

I am starting to get hungry, Jenna Mouse

Sunday: October 26, 2003

Diary, Dearest Diary,

Yesterday, the alarm rang because a mouseling got caught in a small raft in the middle of rapids. We saved him but are still trying to figure out why he was there. Because he is a minor someone had to stay with him until one of his parents got there. I stayed with him and waited several hours while the other E.R.M's tried to get a hold of his parents, and then for his mom to arrive.

When his mom got there, she knew me. I was very confused until she told me how I had saved her son from getting run over in the park parking lot by a skateboarder. Her son is Anole! He has grown so much that I didn't recognize him.

Anole got into even more trouble today. This time, he was stuck in thick mud and couldn't get out. One of the other E.R.M.'s got over anxious and got stuck, too. Kenna stayed with Anole this time. I stayed around for a while talking to the other E.R.M's, and neither of his parents had arrived by the time I left.

There might just be a mystery brewing, Jenna Mouse

Monday: October 27, 2003

Diary, Dearest Diary,

Today, after I got home from running wedding errands, the alarm rang again. The Anole was stuck in the window of a burning shed. A mouse that was passing by saved him, but both of them were severely burned and were hospitalized. Dr. Erma Gensi said that he will have to be there for a week and having some visitors might be good for him.

He hasn't squeaked any word other than "Thank you" these past three days. We can't get him to tell us why he was in the rapids, how he got stuck in the mud, or what happened in the shed.

I have an idea I want to try. I'm thinking Aunt Megan's mouselings are about his age and might be able to get him to tell us something about all of this.

I will go ask for Aunt Megan's permission, Jenna Mouse

Friday: October 31, 2003

Diary, Dearest Diary,

My plan worked! Aunt Megan's mouselings visited Anole in the hospital. The little mouseling wasn't quiet at all with my cousins! He told them that both his parents are always busy and he doesn't get much attention. Then he told them how he was playing in the lake on a raft and got swept into the rapids. His parents gave him so much attention (once they finally arrived) that he decided to get into more 'danger' so that his parents would give him even more affection and attention. How sad, and even his name is even an anagram for "alone".

Minutes before his mom was due home, so he purposely got stuck in the mud outside of their hole. He thought she would be the one to get him out.   She ended up having to work late, and so did his dad. After a long while he started squeaking for help, and a mouse noticed him and called the E.R.M.s

The episode in the burning shed was not exactly his idea… he was going to jump from the window and pretend to have hurt his paw (if he did not for real). He thinks while getting to the window, he might have knocked over something that ended up starting the fire. It spread quickly; and, ironically, he was too afraid to jump!

Later I found out it actually was not Anole's fault that the shed caught on fire. It was an old rundown shed filled with junk, so the owner of the property decided to burn it down so he could use the space it took up to do something else.

Thinking about anagrams; some for Joisinga Anne Noble are "Onion ninja beagles," "One nailing banjoes," and "A neon bonsai jingle."

Tonight we went to Mario's church's fall harvest party. While we were there, it occurred to me that we had not talked about which church we are going to go to as a family. After meeting the mice at Mario's church and hearing the pastor preach a short message, I think that I would like to go to his church.

Mario and his mouselings each dressed up as a different note or other musical sign. Major was a quarter note. Harmony and Melody were connected eight notes. They said that they would never do that again as they fought almost the whole time. One wanted to go left; the other one wanted to go right. One wanted to sit; the other wanted to stand. Ray was a flat, and Lyrical was a sharp. Mario was a treble clef. Mario and I had agreed that he could pick out my costume – I ended up as a bass clef!

I think I like anagrams, Emu On Jeans

Monday: November 10, 2003

Diary, Dearest Diary,

Four more days until I am a married mouse! How exciting! I've worked so hard, yet there always seems to be more to do!

I am going to help Mario's and my parents pick out their wedding clothes today. I think I will suggest to our moms that one of them wear pink and the other one wear brown. Maybe our fathers can wear cream colored suits with a tie to match their wife's dress.

I visited Anole in the hospital the day before he was released and talked to him some about putting himself in danger for attention. I invited him and his family to our church's Christmas mouselings' play, which has cookies and hot apple cider afterwards. The play is on the 14th of December.

I had fun anagramming my married name. I came up with "Romance jets in," which is contrary to "Man rejections." My least favorite was "Cat rejoins men." If Mario and I have a girl, I might suggest we name her Jasmine Cornet, which is all the letters of my married name rearranged. Romeo Stirmica is the best I can come up with for a boy's name from the letters in Mario's name. Maybe I will just stick with Romeo.

Lots to do; so little time, Jenna Mouse

Saturday: November 15, 2003

Diary, Dearest Diary,

I am now married with mouselings! It seems so unreal, yet so natural.

Right before the wedding ceremony Mom reminded me how, on April Fool's Day, I said was getting married on November 14th and would have step-mouselings. Who knew I really would!

Rod was at the wedding with Felicity. They are planning on getting married in Paris on the Eiffel Tower on January 26th, and I am invited. I will have to wait and see if I am available closer to the wedding. Rod was very well mannered for our wedding, like the first time I met him.

Dr. Erma Gensi was there with Terri; I couldn't believe it after how upset he was at me for being an E.R.M. I thought I better warn Dr. Erma about his views, and she said she was already aware of them. When he met Dr. Erma he was taken in by her gentleness, kindness, and beauty. It wasn't until later he learned that she was a doctor. But he decided that, if a woman that wonderful could be a doctor, he didn't mind. It has started in him a new way of thinking.

We are in Memphis, Tennessee, to see Graceland for our honeymoon (the Micestro's are huge fans of Elvis Presley and the mouse that followed him around named Elvis Parsley). And we will visit lots of other attractions. We are staying at In Love Inn which is the mouse hotel inside of Heartbreak Hotel. "In Love Inn" is one of Elvis Parsley's songs.

The only awkward part is the fact that we didn't discuss beforehand what the mouselings would call me. They are still calling me Ms. Jenna. I would never ask them to call me Mom, but I at least wish that they would come up something less formal that they feel comfortable calling me.

Off we go on our new adventure, Jenna Micestro

Tuesday: November 25, 2003

Diary, Dearest Diary,

Graceland was great! We saw and learned lots. We also went the Memphis Zoo, Pink Palace, the Gibson Guitar factory, CMOM, and a few other attractions these past 10 days.

One of the most exciting things for the mouselings was when we went to the Peabody Hotel and got to ride on the ducks, when no one was around of course. And we watched the "Wolf River Pipes and Drums" rehearse at a church in Cordova. My ears are still ringing from the bagpipes. Do you know how loud those things are to mice?

We are also going to visit the Collierville Old Towne Square on Thanksgiving. A battle took place there during the Civil War. Also, off to the side of the working railroad tracks, is an old rail car in which a small area has been converted into a restaurant for mice. We have reservations there for our first Thanksgiving dinner as a family. I will miss not being home with my big family, but this will be something fun and different.

When we get back to Ohio, we will live in Mario's hole. He lives on the street behind the Nobles. In fact, you can see his humans' house from the Nobles upstairs bedroom window. The humans in his house have two children. Their names are Megan and Nathan. I have an aunt and an uncle with the same names!

Everybody is ready to go sightseeing, Jenna Micestro

Wednesday: December 3, 2003

Diary, Dearest Diary,

We're back! On November 29th (I was working since we were home and it was a Saturday) the alarm rang.

A mouse was stuck in a large indoor pool. She knew how to tread water but not how to swim. We pushed the life saver, that was hanging on the wall, out; but the mouse couldn't grip it because it was too big. I happened to notice a human baby teething ring on the floor under a pool chair. I tied some thread around it and tested it, and sure enough it floated. So we used that to save the mouse.

The mouselings are getting anxious for Christmas. Everyday they ask me, "How many more days 'til Christmas?"

It's time to start thinking about Christmas gifts. I suddenly have a lot of mice to buy for! I wonder what my sons might like. Toy cars, comic books, bicycles?!? That's it, bicycles! My Dad and I can make nifty ones out of sticks and acorn tops like we did when I was a mouseling. Then the boys can ride around the house when the humans are not home or when they go to bed.

The girls ought o be easy, hopefully! After all, I have had experience being a girl in my lifetime!

I am going to gather the sticks, Jenna Micestro

Sunday: December 14, 2003

Diary, Dearest Diary,

I did Santa Lucia Day with the girls yesterday. They really enjoyed it. Harmony, who is kinda clumsy, spilled my coffee all over her white dress! But, at least, she wasn't burned since I put just as much milk in mine as I do coffee.

They also liked learning the history behind it. On the twelfth we made Santa Lucia wreath bread at Mom and Dad's hole, while I told the story of Santa Lucia. At the end the girls were crying. The boys pretended they weren't, but I saw tears in the corners of their eyes.

This was Joisinga's first year of being Santa Lucia. She helped her mom make the bread on the twelfth, too. She had dough half way up her arms; it was adorable.

Guess who was at our church Christmas play tonight... Anole and his parents! I told them I am doing a puppet show at church next Sunday. His parents said they might come so Anole can see it.

Dad and I finished the bicycles this afternoon. They look really cool. We used bark and carved out Ray's and Major's names then attached them to the bikes. I really think they will have fun riding them around the house.

Two down; three to left to gift for, Jenna Micestro

Wednesday: December 17, 2003

Diary, Dearest Diary,

I am going to make the girls each a doll for Christmas (I don't mean I am going to turn them into dolls {although with a little makeup I probably could}; I mean I am going to sew dolls for them). Each doll will have different colored fur, eyes, and dresses.

	eyes	fur	dress
Lyrical:	blue	gray	purple
Melody:	green	dark brown	pink
Harmony:	brown	light brown	blue

I need to hurry if I am to get them done in time. I will sew them after the mouselings go to bed. That may mean a few late nights for me!

If they really like how the dresses turn out, it would be a fun project to make each of them a dress to match their dolls, letting them try their paw at sewing.

I need to get fabric, Jenna Micestro

Friday: December 26, 2003

Diary, Dearest Diary,

Merry Late Christmas!

The mouselings loved their presents (in fact, they are playing with them right now).

The mouselings gave me the best gift. They said that, while I could never replace their mom, they would like to call me Momma. They said they feel very blessed to have me in their life.

Anole and his parents came last Sunday, and the whole family became Christians! I hope this helps Anole and his parents with their relationship.

Uh oh, the alarm is ringing, Jenna Micestro

{I'm back}

It wasn't an emergency; they used the alarm to bring us together for a surprise Late Christmas/Early New Year's party. Our families were in on the surprise and left for the station shortly after we did.

We also got awards. My first was the "Helpfulness After the Fact Award". It is because I helped the Micestros after their mother/wife died, and I helped Anole learn not to put himself in danger for attention. Mario presented that award to me.

I also got the "Most Resourceful Award". That one is because I used the teething toy as a life saver and saved Felicity's tail tip. Felicity presented that award to me. It turned out that she had been taking E.R.M. classes and is now a part-time E.R.M. Modeling is still her full-time job.

What a nice end to a nice mice day, Jenna Micestro

Thursday: January 1, 2004

Diary, Dearest Diary,

Happy New Year! Welcome, 2004.

So much has happened in the past year. I worked as a

candy striper and did a puppet show at the hospital. I helped deliver my cousins. I moved into a hole of my own. I helped two of my sisters with their weddings and got two brother-in-laws. I became an E.R.M. and help save many mice. I held a fashion show, had my fashions bought by a store, and saved the homeless shelter with the proceeds from the sales. I set up my sister with her "Mr. Wright". Meanwhile, my other sister set me up with the mouse who turned out to be her Mr. Right. I did the Youth Group class and monthly puppet shows at church with Kenna. I hurt my paw on a mouse trap. I went on a cruise. I helped plan my best friend's wedding.

And last, but far from least, I got married with step-mouselings to boot (and I'm not the old woman who lived in a shoe), went to Memphis on a honeymoon, and moved into another hole. And now I am a part-time E.R.M. (evenings and weekends when Mario is at home to watch the mouselings) and a stay-at-home Mom. I will go back to being a full-time E.R.M. when the mouselings move out. What a crazy year!

At least this year will be calmer...right?

Mario just got home, Jenna Micestro

Monday: January 5, 2004

Diary, Dearest Diary,

I'm pregnant! So much for a calmer year!

I wanted to find a creative way to tell Mario, so I went to the school of music where Mario is a teacher. I gave each of the five mouselings a sheet of poster board, together the posters said, "Momma is having a litter."

We stood outside his classroom window. His guitar student had his back to us, but Mario could see us. Then I had the mouselings one by one walk by the window holding up their sign. He looked very baffled, I then realized they had gotten out of order and it read, "having is litter. a Momma". The boys were in the right places, but the girls had gotten out of order. I rearranged them and had them pass by again.

I think he got the message that time because he passed out. Not realizing we were at the window, his student had no clue as to why he passed out. He stood over Mario for a second, then ran to the sink, filled a cup with water, and poured it on him. That got Mario up quickly!

I went to tell Mom and Dad and met Mom on the way. At once, we both said, "I'm pregnant!" Wow, Mom and I pregnant at the same time, how weird! If Mario passed out, I can't imagine what my dad must have done when Mom told him she was pregnant. We are both due near the middle of this month.

When I told Dad he said, "I know your Mom is... wait! You're pregnant!!!!!!!!!!!" Then he said, "Great, two fussy women at once. I think Mario and I should just leave until the mouselings are born."

When Mario came home from work, he had a bouquet of 5 mini-roses with Baby's Breath. Each of the 5 mini-roses was in the favorite color of one of the mouselings. Everybody is excited. Even Ray and Major said they can't wait to hold the mouselings.

On Sunday, Anole told me his parents have really changed and are now spend a lot of time with him. I learned that his last name is Olives, which is an anagram for "is love".

Now that I am pregnant I can' go to Paris for Felicity's

wedding. But Kenna and Ed are planning on going.

Just days after Christmas, the girls and I started working on dresses for them to match their dolls' dresses. The dresses are coming along nicely, and the girls have learned a lot. Hopefully, they will be willing to help sew outfits and diapers for the mouselings I am having when they are finished with the dresses.

I am going to start preparing, Jenna Micestro

Wednesday: January 14, 2004

Diary Dearest Dairy,

Kenna came over to see the baby stuff this morning and had bad stomach pains. She figured it was because of the spicy tacos she had eaten for brunch.

It wasn't the lunch; she was pregnant! She gave birth to one little girl mouseling at noon. Good thing both of us are E.R.M.s. It was scary, yet exciting to help my best friend give birth. Outside of her stomach pains, it was an easy birth. She never even squeaked out in pain. This experience has made me less nervous about my own delivery.

When Ed came to pick her up, he asked me, "Oh, did you deliver your mouseling prematurely?" I could only smile.

Kenna said, "No, this little bundle of joy is ours!"

All Ed could say was, "uh, uh, um, wha-, huh?" I loved that he was reduced to similar words to those I used on our only date!

Since she didn't even know she was pregnant, she and Ed had not talked about names. They will decide what to name her later. I wonder what kind of names you can anagram from sesquipedalian? Regardless of what they decide, I am sure it will be interesting, just like they are.

Kenna is excited, but bummed, that now she can't go to Paris for Felicity's wedding. She said she would pick this baby over going to Paris any day!

Things have been crazy getting ready for our mouselings. The older ones are excited but nervous;

they have expressed concern over whether or not it will change their dad's feelings for them. It reminds me of when I came into their family. I have assured them over and over that neither his nor my feelings will change for them – they are loved very much.

The girls and I spend hours sewing little outfits and diapers - lots of diapers! The girls love adding lots of lace to the clothes. I had to stop them when they tried to add it to the diapers as well! With some of the outfits, I'm not even sure if we will be able to see the mouselings hiding under the lace!

Lyrical just hurt herself with a needle, Jenna Micestro

Saturday: January 17, 2004

Diary Dearest Dairy,

I think the mouselings are coming! Jenna Micestro

{With the new arrivals}

Jasmine, Jasper, Ramona, Romeo, Norma, and Norman have arrived. Jasmine is the only one with a middle name, you guessed it, Cornet!

I am going to catch up on my sleep, Jenna Misestro

[Still at the hospital}

You'll never believe who's here... Mom! And she didn't just come to see her first grand-mouselings; she's in labor! Well, they actually did come to see the mouselings; but while they were here holding their grand-mouselings Mom went into labor! I wanted to be with Mom. They nurses said they had never had a case like this, so Mom and I are in hospital beds right next to each other!

I think Mom is about to give birth, Jenna Micestro

{Even later}

Mom has just given me four more beautiful siblings! Their names are Maria, Mario, Justin, and Justice.

Justin, Justice, and Mario are my first (and only) brothers. Mario (my husband) loved Mario's (my brother's) name!

Mario is bringing the older mouselings, Jenna Micestro

Wednesday: February 4, 2004

Diary, Dearest Diary,

They mouselings are now covered with fur and are much more independent.

The mouselings have been keeping me busy, but I made time to write today since it is Joisinga's and many of my aunts' and uncles' birthday. They are all turning four.

The mouselings are getting bigger by the day. All too soon they'll stop being babies! I am enjoying every minute of it before its gone! The older mouselings fell in love with the younger ones as soon as they met them.

On the 28th of January, Kenna's mouseling opened her eyes. They were green, so Ed and Kenna named her Esmeralda, which means Emerald. Her full name is Esmeralda Kandra Edwina Ward.

Mom's mouselings, my mouselings, and Esmeralda will often play together. Maria, Ramona, and Esmeralda have become close buddies.

The mouselings are crying, Jenna Micestro

Sunday: February 8, 2004

Diary, Dearest Diary,

Joisinga just had the COOLEST birthday party yesterday. Its theme was Angelina Ballerina. Angelina is a cartoon character, who is a white mouse with a pink tutu. Mr. Noble dressed up as Angelina in a 6 foot tall mouse costume. Despite his size, he doesn't make that bad of a mouse.

Mr. and Mrs. Noble invited just about every one of their family and friends. They asked for people not to bring gifts, but to bring a potluck dish instead. They were able to feed so many people that way. Joisinga had 2 cakes. One was Angelina and the other was Alice, her best friend.

They did so much to decorate and plan for this party. They created a "ballet class room" from the front door to, and around, the eat-in space complete with ballet bars and mirrors. Mrs. Noble made poster board mice from the cartoon series and placed them around on the mirrors.

The living room had lots of pink, white, and green balloons, and that's where most of the adults sat and talked. The basement was cleared of all toys and that's where "Angelina" read some stories to the kids and played some games. "Angelina" was also back later to take pictures with everyone.

All the girls got a white stuffed mouse that had a pink tutu as a gift. The boys got a tan bear stuffed toy.

Six more days until my 2nd birthday, Jenna Micestro

Saturday: February 14, 2004

Diary, Dearest Diary,

Happy Valentines Day! And Happy Birthday to my litter! And Happy Anniversary to Aunt Julia and Uncle Ernst!

It is a family tradition to pick a sibling to be your Valentine and get a gift for that mouse. I picked Maria. She is really advanced for her age and can already read and write. So I got her a diary and matching pen. She seems thrilled about it, in fact she started writing in it right away (or should I say 'write away' ha ha)!

For my birthday, Mario composed a song for me. Melody played the piano, Lyrical played the harp, Harmony played violin, Major played the flute, and Ray played French Horn. Mario serenaded me as they played; he held my hand and we danced around the room as he sang. It was beautiful. I have no idea where they found the time to practice. Mario also had his original composition of it framed for me. It is called, ""Für Jenna."

All eleven of our mouselings fell asleep about an hour ago (and then Jasmine Cornet woke up, but she is back asleep now) so Mario and I are going to have dinner by candle light. He and I ate lightly during our family dinner, which was hard since it was extra cheesy pizza with pepperonis cut into the shape of hearts.

We are going to have chocolate dipped strawberries for an appetizer, four cheese and spinach quiche (or as we like to call it "Quiche the Cook") for dinner, and for dessert "Cobble Road Cobbler" (a peach and apple cobbler, and cinnamon is in it as well). As a surprise I made more of our special wedding tea blend of white tea leaves, white peach, apple, and a hint of cinnamon.

Time for a romantic night with Mario, Jenna Micestro

Monday: February 23, 2004

Diary, Dearest Diary,

The mouselings said their first word today. You'll never believe what it was, "Ice cream," although it sounded more like "Iz-ceam!" It is rather unusual for all the mouselings to say their first word all at once. It was while I was dishing up bowls of chocolate ice cream for the older mouselings. It was so cute that I decided to give them each a small bowl, too.

Norma just hurt Ramona, Jenna Micestro

Sunday: February 29, 2004

Diary, Dearest Diary,

Happy Leap Day!

The mouselings are almost six weeks old. And they are growing big and strong - all except for Ramona. She is the smallest and weakest (she is the runt). Sometimes her siblings will try to take advantage of her size, but I reprimand that kind of behavior. Maria is also the runt of her litter. Esmeralda is tiny as well. The three of them together are adorable.

The older mouselings love to help teach the little ones. I don't mind because that just means less work for me. Actually, it is really good bonding time for them; and I can get hole work done.

The mouselings are out-growing all of their clothes, so while the boys watch the mouselings the girls and I sew new clothes for them. Last time we were sewing, Norma slipped away from the boys and got a hold of a needle. One of the girls noticed just in time and saved her from hurting herself.

I have been taking a maternity leave from being an E.R.M since the mouselings were born. I don't miss the excitement; I get enough at home! It's almost easier to be an E.R.M. than to be a mom!

Soap suds on the floor!?! Uh-oh!, Jenna Micestro

{After taking care of the 'clean mess'}

Melody and Harmony were supposed to be watching the young ones, but yet the mouselings managed to get the bar of hand soap. They sloshed water on the floor and used the soap to make it sudsy. What a 'clean mess'!

It reminded me of when Aunt Megan stayed with Mrs. Dorothy when her hole was being remodeled for all the mouselings she was adopting...what am I in for?

Mom said Maria is even more of a trouble maker. She said that she had to reprimand her this morning for jumping all over, and she is always getting in trouble for one thing after another. On the 17th, Kenna took Esmaralda, Ramona, and Maria to the movies and the girls showed up with bells hung on their ears!

I better help watch the mouselings, Jenna Micestro

Wednesday: March 3, 2004

Diary, Dearest Diary,

Mario is watching the mouselings for the day so I can spend a girl's day with Kenna, Harmony, Melody, and Lyrical. I can't wait for Kenna to get here so I can get a break! Although I am a little nervous about leaving six mouselings and three men alone; it could end in a catastrophe!

Kenna's here!!!!!!!!!!!!!!!, Jenna Micestro

Wednesday: March 17, 2004

Diary, Dearest Diary,

Happy St. Patrick's Day! The younger mouselings asked me what St. Patrick's Day was about and I told them the story about St. Patrick using a shamrock to teach about the Trinity, Three-in-One.

Since the Santa Lucia wreath bread was a big hit with the older mouselings last December, I decided to make shamrock shaped sugar cookies with the younger mouselings. I let them ice the cookies, with green icing, of course! There was much icing on them as there was on the cookies by the time they were done.

We are going to have more green food, Jenna Micestro

Wednesday: March 24, 2004

Diary, Dearest Diary,

I just began teaching the mouselings to read. Some of them hate it, and the others love it! I have a love of reading; and I hope they will, too.

I think I will motivate them by having them read 'If You Give a Mouse a Cookie' and letting them act out the story with real cookies and other props.

I am going to go bake the cookies now, Jenna Micestro

Wednesday: March 31, 2004

Diary, Dearest Diary,

My plan worked; the cookies motivated them to read! They acted out the story and asked if they could do it again for Mario. I let them. After the second time they were full of sugar that they were bouncing off of the walls (that's not in the story!). Maybe I should have thought it through before saying yes to the second time...

I am going to help teach the mouselings how to read some more words, words without sugar that is.

Ready to read or not here I come, Jenna Micestro

Sunday: April 4, 2004

Diary, Dearest Diary

I hardly have time to write any more, which works out well since I am running out of space in my Diary, so this is au revoir.

I told you in December of 2002 that I would have a lot of adventures to share with you, and I think I did just that. While my life is no longer full of exciting E.R.M. adventures and now I am a stay-at-home, home-schooling mom, it's still an adventure every day for me. Maybe when the mouselings are older, I can go back to being a full-time E.R.M. (unless I do what my mom did and have another litter after all our mouselings are married off – yikes, what am I saying?!).

Megan came home from her dance class, that she recently started going, to talking about a girl named Joisinga. I always thought they would make good friends.

Goodbye, Adios, Adieu, Hej då, Jenna Micestro

Made in the USA
Charleston, SC
08 August 2014